D0938267

To JULIA IRIS FOREVER...

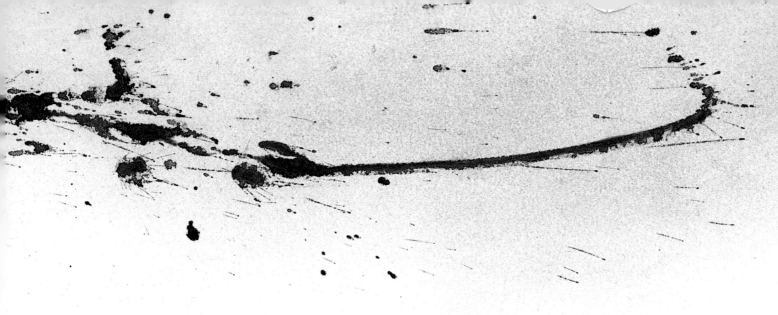

STEPHEN GAMMELL

Mudkin

CAROLRHODA BOOKS · MINNEAPOLIS

RAIN'S GONE... YOUR QUEEN
COMMANDS THAT WE ALL
GO OUT and PLAY!

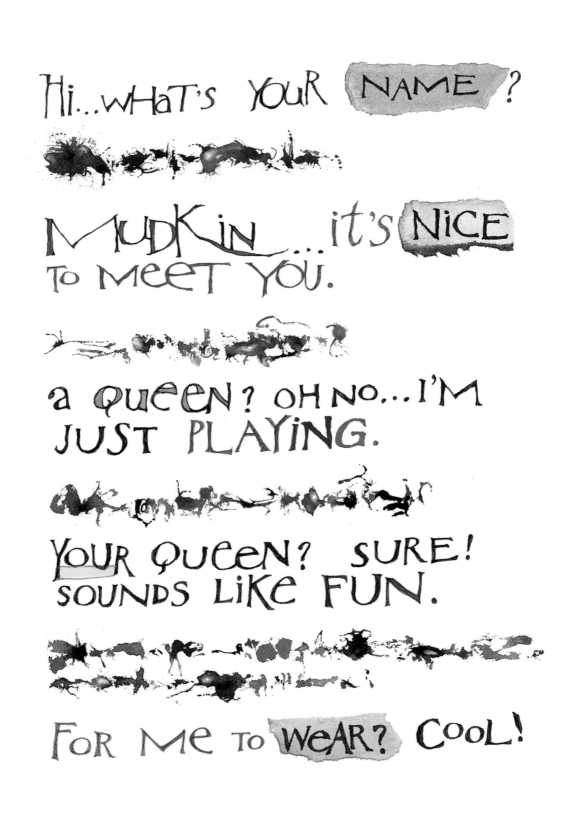

Hi...WHAT'S YOUR NAME?

MUDKIN ...it's NICE TO MEET YOU.

a QUEEN? OH NO...I'M JUST PLAYING.

YOUR QUEEN? SURE! SOUNDS LIKE FUN.

FOR ME TO WEAR? COOL!

WOW! YOU REALLY MEAN IT?

OH MY... THERE'S SO
MANY OF YOU!

YES, ALWAYS. FOREVER...

Carolrhoda Books
A division of Lerner Publishing Group, Inc.
241 First Avenue North
Minneapolis, MN 55401 U.S.A.

Website address: www.lernerbooks.com

Library of Congress Cataloging-in-Publication Data

Gammell, Stephen.
    Mudkin / by Stephen Gammell ; illustrated by Stephen Gammell.
       p.   cm.
    Summary: While playing outside on a rainy day, a little girl peers into a puddle and sees Mudkin, who invites her to become his queen.
    ISBN: 978-0-7613-5790-2 (lib. bdg. : alk. paper)
    [1. Play—Fiction. 2. Mud—Fiction. 3. Imagination—Fiction. 4. Rain and rainfall—Fiction.] I. Title.
PZ7.G144Mud 2011
[E]—dc22   2010026373

Manufactured in the United States of America
1 — DP — 12/31/10